Dora the Explorer
Super Babies Dream Adventure

adapted by Christine Ricci
based on the screenplay written by Jorge Aguirre
illustrated by Dave Aikins

SIMON AND SCHUSTER/NICKELODEON

Based on the TV series Dora the Explorer™ as seen on Nick Jr.™

Simon and Schuster
First published in Great Britain in 2010 by Simon & Schuster UK Ltd
1st Floor, 222 Gray's Inn Road, London WC1X 8HB
A CBS Company

A CIP catalogue record for this book is available from the British Library

ISBN 978-1-84738-769-1
Printed in Great Britain

10 9 8 7 6 5 4 3 2 1

Visit our websites:
www.simonandschuster.co.uk
www.nickjr.co.uk

¡Hola! I'm Dora, and this is Boots. It's nap time for my baby brother, Guillermo, and my baby sister, Isabella. I always tell them a story before they fall asleep. They love stories about the Super Babies. Do you want to hear the story? Great!

Once upon a time there was a Dream Fairy who could only be woken up by the sound of her Golden Rooster. When the rooster yelled "¡Ki-ki-ri-ki!," the Dream Fairy would wake up and deliver happy dreams to all of the babies.

One day the Super Babies didn't get their nap-time dreams. Using their supersight to see through the forest, they discovered that all of the babies were still awake! None of the babies could nap until the Dream Fairy brought them their dreams!

What could have happened to the Dream Fairy? We've got to find her so that all of the babies can have their nap-time dreams. Who do we ask for help when we don't know which way to go? Map!

Map says that the Dream Fairy is asleep in the Dream Castle and can't hear the Golden Rooster. We'll need to go past the Giant's Forest and over Dragon Mountain to get to the Dream Fairy's Castle. ¡Vámonos! Let's go!

Look! There's Tico! He's trying to rock three baby chipmunks to sleep. But the babies don't have their dreams yet. They can't fall asleep and they're cranky! I know how we can make the chipmunks happy! Will you sing "Twinkle, Twinkle, Little Star" to the baby chipmunks?

Twinkle, twinkle, little star,
how I wonder what you are!
Up above the world so high,
like a diamond in the sky!
Twinkle, twinkle, little star . . .

Your singing made the baby chipmunks smile!

Now, we're in the Giant's Forest, and I can hear crying. Can you see who's crying? It's a giant baby, and the wind is rocking his cradle. Oh, no! The cradle might fall!

The Super Babies will rescue the Giant Baby. Let's help the Super Babies superblow the windy cloud away.

Take a deep breath in and *blOW!*

Great job! We blew the windy cloud away. Look! The Super Babies are superlifting the Giant Baby out of the tree.

Now we need to find Dragon Mountain. Can you see Dragon Mountain?

There it is! Come on! Let's go to the Dream Castle so that we can wake up the Dream Fairy. Then the babies can get their nap-time dreams.

Dragon Mountain is so steep! Luckily the Super Babies can superfly us to the top of the mountain. Oh, no! The Super Babies ripped their blankets. They can't fly without their blankets.

Hey, that's my friend, Camila. Camila's *mami* taught her how to make blankets in Guatemala. She can help us fix the Super Babies' blankets. Let's go inside their shop!

Look! The diamonds on Isabella's blanket follow a pattern. The pattern is: rojo, azul, rojo, azul, rojo . . . what comes next? ¡Azul! That's right! Blue!

Camila can use her loom to weave a blue diamond. She fixed the rip!

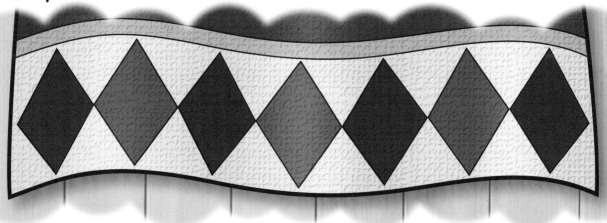

Now let's look at Guillermo's blanket. The diamonds on his blanket have a pattern too. The pattern is: azul, azul, rojo, azul, azul, rojo, azul, azul . . . what comes next? ¡Rojo! Yes! Red!

Camila weaves a red diamond over the rip. Camila fixed the Super Babies' blankets!

Now the Super Babies are superflying us to the top of Dragon Mountain. Oh, no! Those baby dragons won't let us go by. They are so cranky! Maybe they need a nap-time snack?

Baby dragons love red chili peppers. Do you see a red chili pepper plant? Great! Now let's count in Spanish how many baby dragons there are.

¡Uno, dos, tres, cuatro, cinco, seis, siete, ocho, nueve, diez, once, doce! The twelve baby dragons love their red chili pepper snack! They are letting us go over their mountain!

We made it to the Dream Castle, and there's the Dream Fairy! Is she awake or asleep? Asleep! To help the Golden Rooster wake up the Dream Fairy, we have to yell, "¡Ki-ki-ri-ki!"

We woke up the Dream Fairy! Now she needs our help to deliver all of the dreams before nap time is over. Come on! We can superfly superfast with the Super Babies!

To deliver dreams to all of the babies in the forest, we need to wish them sweet dreams. In Spanish we say "¡Dulces sueños!"
Look! Now all of the babies are having sweet dreams!

The baby dragons have chili pepper dreams. The giant baby has bunny dreams, and the baby chipmunks have twinkle-star dreams . . .

The Dream Fairy saved two special dreams for the Super Babies. Guillermo is dreaming of a clown, and Isabella is dreaming about puppies!

Thanks for helping us wake up the Dream Fairy and bring happy nap-time dreams to all of the babies! May all your dreams be sweet! ¡Dulces sueños!